HOLLY MUN

A Boy and His Blue Dog

AuthorHouse™ UK
1663 Liberty Drive
Bloomington, IN 47403 USA
www.authorhouse.co.uk
UK TFN: 0800 0148641 (Toll Free inside the UK)
UK Local: 02036 956322 (+44 20 3695 6322 from outside the UK)

Because of the dynamic nature of the Internet, any web addresses or links contained in this book may have changed since publication and may no longer be valid. The views expressed in this work are solely those of the author and do not necessarily reflect the views of the publisher, and the publisher hereby disclaims any responsibility for them.

Any people depicted in stock imagery provided by Getty Images are models, and such images are being used for illustrative purposes only. Certain stock imagery © Getty Images.

This book is printed on acid-free paper.

ISBN: 978-1-6655-9009-9 (sc)
ISBN: 978-1-6655-9008-2 (e)

Print information available on the last page.

Published by AuthorHouse 05/25/2021

authorHOUSE®

A BOY AND HIS BLUE DOG

HOLLY MUNNS

Thank you to my family, without whom
my dreams would seem out of reach
And to My Dad for being
my inspiration, always.

A young blue-eyed boy called Nick lived in a tiny timbered cottage. He had a very special friend called Solo. Solo had four legs and a big wet nose—and Solo was blue. They were the best of friends and loved to explore together. On today's adventure, Nick wanted to go and see their wildlife friends, so off the two of them went.

In their garden was a big pond full of muddy green water where Nick and Solo most loved to play. When they got there, Captain Carp was swimming in circles around a lily pad.

"What are you doing, Captain Carp?" asked Nick.

"Lucy's lily pad has been empty all morning," said Captain Carp. "She's missing!"

"She must have gone for some breakfast and got lost," said Nick.

"If we work together, we can find her!" barked Solo, and he put his big wet nose to the ground and started sniffing.

"What's that dog doing?" asked Captain Carp.

Nick laughed. "Dogs have a very good sense of smell, and he's going to see if he can smell where Lucy went."

And off the three of them went: Captain Carp swimming, Solo sniffing, and Nick marching.

Not long after, they bumped into a friend called Burt, a grumpy goose.

"Maybe Bert can help us find Lucy," said Captain Carp, "as geese have amazing eyesight and can see things much farther away than we can."

Nick thought that was a great idea. "Hi, Bert! We are trying to find Lucy. Can you help us?"

In a slow grumpy voice, Bert honked, "I guess I can help. There's not much else to do around here."

So off the four of them went: Captain Carp swimming, Solo sniffing, Nick marching, and Bert waddling behind.

Around the pond they went until they discovered a rock. This rock was too heavy for Nick to pick up alone, but together as a team they thought they could move it. Nick undid the laces on his shoes and tied them to the rock. Captain Carp took one end, Bert the next, and Solo the other. Nick pulled his end of the lace as hard as he could.

"Pull!" shouted Nick. All the friends pulled together until the rock started to move.

"It's moving! Keep going," said Captain Carp.

They pulled and pulled and eventually the rock rolled over. A small squeak came from under the rock.

Bert honked, "Polly, is that you?"

"Yes, it's me," said Polly in an angry voice. "Hedgehogs sleep through the day, you know"

"Sorry," said Nick, "but we've lost Lucy. Can you help us find her?"

"I saw Lucy early this morning, near that log over there," said Polly as she pointed to the other side of the pond.

So off the five of them went: Captain Carp swimming, Solo sniffing, Nick marching, Bert waddling, and Polly scurrying behind.

They reached the log and started to search.

"It was here where I saw Lucy last," said Polly.

In a slow grumpy voice, Bert honked, "There's nothing here but a pair of Nick's old wellies."

Suddenly Solo went whizzing off with his nose to the ground.

"What is it, boy?" said Nick, chasing after him.

Solo barked and stuck his head in Nick's welly.

"Lucy must be in there!" Nick shouted. "Lucy?" He took the welly off Solo's head and looked inside. "There you are! We've been looking everywhere for you."

Lucy looked very happy to see everyone. "I got stuck in here this morning when I was looking for breakfast."

"That was silly," Bert honked.

"We are happy we've found you safe and sound," said Polly. "Now let's get you back to your lily pad."

"Good idea," Captain Carp said. "After all, there is no place like home."

"This has been a great adventure," said Nick, "but all this talk is making me sleepy."

"Me too!" honked Bert.

Lucy smiled. "I have the best of friends."

"Great friends we all are," declared Captain Carp.

"And always will be," added Polly.

Solo licked Nick's face. Nick laughed. "Let's go home."

And off the six of them went ...

ABOUT THE AUTHOR

A Boy and His Blue Dog is very special to me as it is my first children's book and has been written on behalf of my dad, who described this story to me many years ago.

I hope you enjoy reading this book as much as I have enjoyed writing it.

Thank you to my family, without whom my dreams would seem out of reach.

And to My Dad for being my inspiration, always.